Jessica's ne

"I want to know why you repeated the things I told you," I said. "You made my friends mad at me."

"So?" Jessica Farrell said.

"So I don't like it when my friends are mad!" I told her.

"So?" Jessica Farrell said.

"So you'd better stop!" I yelled.

Jessica Farrell shook her head. "You can't tell me what to do. In fact, you better leave me alone—or else."

"Or else what?" I asked.

"Or else I'll tell the rest of what you told me," Jessica Farrell said. "Then you won't have any friends at all."

Bantam Books in the SWEET VALLEY KIDS series

SWEET VALLEY KIDS

JESSICA + JESSICA = TROUBLE

Written by
Molly Mia Stewart

Created by
FRANCINE PASCAL

Illustrated by
Ying-Hwa Hu

BANTAM BOOKS
NEW YORK•TORONTO•LONDON•SYDNEY•AUCKLAND

RL 2, 005-008

JESSICA + JESSICA = TROUBLE
A Bantam Book / June 1995

Sweet Valley High® and Sweet Valley Kids are
trademarks of Francine Pascal

Conceived by Francine Pascal

Produced by Daniel Weiss Associates, Inc.
33 West 17th Street
New York, NY 10011

Cover art by Susan Tang

ISBN: 0-553-48211-4

Published simultaneously in the United States and Canada

Bantam Books are published by Bantam Books, a division of Bantam
Doubleday Dell Publishing Group, Inc. Its trademark, consisting of the
words "Bantam Books" and the portrayal of a rooster, is Registered in the
U.S. Patent and Trademark Office and in other countries.   Marca
Registrada. Bantam Books, 1540 Broadway, New York, New York 10036.

PRINTED IN THE UNITED STATES OF AMERICA

OPM   0 9 8 7 6 5 4 3 2 1

To Anders Johansson

CHAPTER 1

Student of the Week

Hi! My name is Jessica Wakefield. I am seven years old.

My twin sister, Elizabeth, is also seven years old. We have the same birthday. We also share the same room. That's because we are identical twins. We look just like each other! Elizabeth has blue-green eyes like mine. We both have long blond hair with bangs. Elizabeth likes to wear her hair in a ponytail a lot. I only wear a ponytail when I want to match my sister.

I also dress like Elizabeth when we want to match. We have a bunch of clothes that look alike. When we wear the same outfit, nobody can tell who is who. We fool our friends. Sometimes we fool Mom and Dad and our big brother, Steven.

Elizabeth and I are in the same class at Sweet Valley Elementary School. We are in second grade, and our teacher is Mrs. Otis.

I like school because I see all of my friends there. We play together at recess and pass notes during class. Mrs. Otis doesn't like when we pass notes. Neither does Elizabeth. She likes to pay attention and learn. She even likes to do her homework! I don't think homework is any fun at all.

My best friends (after Elizabeth) are Ellen Riteman and Lila Fowler. We all like to play with dolls and wear pretty clothes. Elizabeth's favorite friends are Amy Sutton and Todd Wilkins. They play tag and dodgeball on the playground.

I'm not a tomboy, like Elizabeth. On the playground my favorite thing is jump rope. That's because I jump rope better than anyone in my whole class.

Lots of people think that Elizabeth and I should be exactly like each other. But just because we look the same doesn't mean we *are* the same. After all, there's only one Jessica Wakefield.

Elizabeth and I share a lot of things. But sometimes things can't be shared. The Student of the Week contest is like that. Only one person can be Student of the Week at a time. Mrs. Otis started the Student of the Week contest last Friday. This is how it works:

Every Friday morning, everyone in our class writes a paper about why another kid has been great that week. We each get to pick who we want to write about. The student described in the best paper gets his or her picture put

3

up on the bulletin board. So does the person who wrote the best paper.

Elizabeth was the first Student of the Week. Eva had written about her. I was sure I would be the second Student of the Week. But that was before I met Ellen's cousin.

"All right!" I exclaimed on Monday morning. "It's time for my favorite class."

Mrs. Otis was leading us down the hall to the playground. I was walking with Ellen and Lila. Elizabeth was ahead of us. She was walking with Amy.

"Recess is your favorite class?" Lila asked me.

"Yup," I said.

Lila giggled. But Ellen didn't even smile.

"I want to play hopscotch," Lila announced.

"OK," I agreed.

Ellen didn't say anything.

Mrs. Otis opened the door that leads outside. The entire class rushed out onto the playground. Lila and I ran to the closest hopscotch board to save it.

Ellen followed us. She was walking slowly.

"Hurry up!" Lila called to Ellen.

Ellen didn't walk any faster.

"What's wrong with you?" Lila demanded when Ellen finally caught up with us.

"You've been quiet all morning," I added.

"I'm in a bad mood," Ellen said.

That was easy to see. Ellen had her arms crossed. A giant frown was on her face.

"How come?" I asked.

"My cousin is coming to visit," Ellen said. "Mom and Dad are making me bring her to school with me the rest of the week."

"I think visitors are fun," I said.

"Some visitors are fun," Ellen agreed. "But not Jessica. I can't stand her."

I was surprised. Why was Ellen mad at *me*?

Ellen noticed the look on my face. "My cousin's name is Jessica, too," she explained. "Jessica Farrell."

"That's so cool!" I exclaimed.

Ellen frowned.

I wanted to say that meeting another Jessica would be neat. Jessica Farrell and I probably had a lot in common. But I bit my tongue. Ellen didn't like her cousin. I wouldn't tell Ellen I couldn't wait to meet the other Jessica. That would just make her mad.

"How old is your cousin?" I asked.

"Our age," Ellen said.

"Why don't you like her?" Lila asked.

"Last time she visited, my whole family got mad at me," Ellen said. "Now she's going to come to school.

And I'm sure everyone here will get mad at me."

Lila and I traded surprised looks.

"Listen," I told Ellen. "Don't worry about Jessica. She won't be here until tomorrow. Let's play hopscotch."

"You play." Ellen still looked grumpy.

Lila shrugged. "OK. Come on, Jess."

I was about to join Lila and play without Ellen. But then I remembered the Student of the Week contest. Maybe if I cheered Ellen up, she would write about me on Friday.

What will make Ellen happy? I asked myself. She usually liked hopscotch. But I knew it wasn't her favorite game. Jump rope was.

"Hey, did you guys see the International Jump Rope Finals on TV last night?" I asked.

"I saw it," Ellen said with a little smile. "It was super cool."

"I saw it too," Lila said.

7

"The double Dutch was the best part," Ellen said.

Lila and I both nodded.

"I wish we could do that," Ellen added.

"Let's try," I suggested.

"All right!" Ellen was really grinning now.

Lila wasn't. "I thought we were going to play hopscotch."

"We can," I said. "Later."

"But I don't want to play double Dutch," Lila said.

I took Ellen's hand. "Then we'll see you later," I told Lila.

Lila looked mad. But I didn't pay any attention. I knew there was no chance Lila would write about me on Friday. She'd written about me the week before. One of the contest rules was you couldn't write about the same person two weeks in a row. Ellen and I ran over to the swings. Elizabeth, Amy, and Eva Simpson were swinging.

"Hey, Elizabeth!" I yelled. "Want to play double Dutch?"

"No, thanks!" Elizabeth doesn't like jump rope.

I thought fast. "I have to tell you a secret," I yelled to Elizabeth.

"Sure." Elizabeth put her feet down and stopped her swing.

Ellen waited while I ran over to Elizabeth.

"I need your help," I whispered in Elizabeth's ear. "Ellen's in a bad mood. I'm trying to cheer her up. She wants to jump rope. But we need three people."

"OK, I'll play," Elizabeth agreed immediately. I knew she would. Elizabeth loves to do good deeds.

Ellen, Elizabeth, and I got a jump rope from Mr. Butler. He's our gym teacher. He's always on the playground during recess.

"We'd better figure out how to turn it first," Elizabeth said.

"No problem," I said.

Well, it turned out to be a *little* problem. Double Dutch is much harder than plain old jump rope. Both turners have to hold a piece of rope in each hand. First they turn one side, and then the other.

Ellen and Elizabeth turned first. It took them a while to figure out how to do it right.

I could tell jumping double Dutch would be more difficult, too. I'd have to jump twice as fast as usual.

"OK, Jessica," Ellen finally called. "Ready when you are."

I ran in . . . and tripped on the rope right away.

"My turn," Ellen said.

I took the rope from her. Elizabeth and I started to turn.

Ellen ran in . . . and tripped. She got up and took the rope from Elizabeth. "Good luck," she said.

Elizabeth ran in. She jumped for about two seconds. Then her feet got tangled in the rope. She fell on her bottom—hard.

"Are you OK?" Ellen called.

Elizabeth didn't answer.

"Lizzie?" I said.

There were tears in Elizabeth's eyes. But she didn't cry. She got up and brushed off her pants. I felt proud. Elizabeth's tough.

Eva and Amy ran up.

"Can we watch?" Eva asked.

"Sure," Elizabeth said.

Ellen, Elizabeth, and I each tried again. We all fell.

"Want to go?" I asked Ellen.

"No," she said. "I've had enough."

"Do you guys want a turn?" I asked Amy and Eva.

They each shook their head.

"Do you want to go?" Elizabeth asked me.

"Sure." I stood near the swinging rope. I listened to the pattern of sound the rope made when it hit the ground. Thump-thump. Thump-thump. Thump-thump. When I ran in, I had the beat. I jumped and jumped without tripping. When the bell rang, I ran out and didn't fall.

"You were great," Elizabeth said as we wound up the rope. "I wish I could do that."

"You could," I said. "You just have to keep trying."

"I'm going to," Elizabeth said.

"At lunch?" I asked.

"No." Elizabeth frowned. "I think I'm tripping because of my shoes. I want to change them before I try again. Let's do it tomorrow."

"OK," I agreed.

We lined up. Mrs. Otis started to lead us into school.

Eva was right behind me. "I'm going to write about you on Friday," she told me.

"You are?" I asked.

Eva nodded. "I think you should be Student of the Week."

"Why?" I asked.

"Because you jump rope so well," Eva said.

I grinned.

CHAPTER 2

The Jessica Connection

"Jessica, this is Jessica," Ellen said on Tuesday morning. "Jessica, meet Jessica."

I giggled.

So did Jessica Farrell.

Jessica and I had the same name, but we didn't look anything alike. Jessica Farrell had long red hair, and about a billion freckles.

"Great shoes," Jessica Farrell told me.

I glanced down at my pink Keds. "Thanks."

"And that bracelet is really cool," Jessica Farrell added.

"Thanks," I said again.

"Hi!" It was Elizabeth.

"Hi, Elizabeth," I said. "This is Ellen's cousin. Her name is Jessica, just like mine."

Jessica Farrell's eyes were wide. "You guys are so lucky to be twins!"

Elizabeth smiled. "We know."

"You and I are twins too," I told Jessica Farrell. "Name twins!"

"Hey, you're right," Jessica Farrell said. "That's cool."

Ellen rolled her eyes.

Mrs. Otis came up to us.

"This is my cousin," Ellen told her.

"I've been expecting you," Mrs. Otis said to Jessica Farrell. "We're looking forward to having you in our class this week. Let's find a seat for you before class begins."

"OK," Jessica Farrell agreed.

"Lila, why don't you move to the back row?" Mrs. Otis suggested. Lila's desk is between Ellen's and mine.

"Do I have to?" Lila asked. The only open seat in the back row was next to Jim Sturbridge. Jim's not that bad. But he is a *boy*.

"It's only for a few days," Mrs. Otis told Lila.

Lila got up and stomped toward the back of the room.

Mrs. Otis smiled at Jessica Farrell. "You can have Lila's place."

I was happy I got to sit next to Jessica Farrell. As soon as we sat down, I passed her a note. Jessica Farrell read it, wrote something, and passed the note back. We passed notes for almost an hour.

Guess what? I was right! Jessica Farrell and I *did* have a lot in common. We both loved tuna-fish sandwiches and hopscotch. We agreed Winston Egbert had the ugliest ears in class.

Later that morning, we had art.

Jessica Farrell and I sat next to each other. Ellen and Lila were also at our table. They were coloring a huge picture together.

"Please pass the purple crayon, Jessica," I said.

"Here you are, Jessica," Jessica Farrell said.

"Thank you, Jessica."

"You're welcome, Jessica."

Jessica Farrell and I giggled.

Ellen and Lila traded disgusted looks.

"Purple is my favorite color," I told Jessica Farrell.

"Mine too," she said.

"Shh!" Ellen said.

"It's art," I reminded Ellen. "We don't have to be quiet."

"Well, you're still talking too much," Ellen said. "I can't think!" She stood up, picked up her drawing, and moved to another table.

17

"Hey!" Lila said. "That's my drawing too."

Ellen didn't turn around.

Lila shrugged. She got up and followed Ellen. They sat down at Elizabeth's table.

"I'd better go see what's wrong," I told Jessica Farrell.

"OK," she said.

I walked over to the other table.

"Are you mad at me?" I asked Ellen.

"No," Ellen said. "Well, sort of. You shouldn't be so buddy-buddy with Jessica. She's not as nice as she seems."

"I'll watch out," I told Ellen. But secretly I thought she was being silly. Maybe she was jealous of her cousin.

"Is Ellen OK?" Jessica Farrell asked when I got back to our table.

"Sure," I said.

"She's so lucky," Jessica Farrell said. "Sweet Valley is great. And I love Mrs. Otis's class."

19

"Me, too," I said.

"Who are your best friends?" Jessica Farrell asked.

"Elizabeth and Lila and Ellen," I said.

"Molly is my best friend at home," Jessica Farrell said. "We have lots of fun together. But sometimes we fight."

"It's the same with me and my friends," I said. "But we always make up."

"What do you and Ellen fight about?" Jessica asked.

I shrugged. "Stupid stuff."

"Like what?" Jessica Farrell asked.

"Once Ellen got mad because I beat her in hopscotch every day for two weeks," I said. "She kept messing up on the number-eight square."

Jessica Farrell giggled. "Do you ever fight with Lila?"

"Sure," I said.

"What about?" Jessica Farrell asked.

"Once I found out a secret about

her," I said. "Lila got mad because she didn't want anyone to know."

"What did you find out?" Jessica Farrell asked.

"Well . . ." I said.

"Come on," Jessica Farrell said. "You can tell me."

"I don't know if I should," I said.

Jessica Farrell looked mad. "Fine."

I felt bad. I didn't want to fight with my new friend. Besides, I was sure I could trust her.

"OK," I said. "I'll tell you."

Jessica Farrell's face brightened.

I leaned closer to whisper in her ear.

CHAPTER 3

New Shoes

"**D**o you want to play tag?" Jessica Farrell asked me during morning recess.

I wrinkled my nose and shook my head. "I hate tag."

"Me too," Jessica Farrell said quickly.

I gave Jessica Farrell a funny look. If she hated tag, why did she ask if I wanted to play? It was weird. Maybe she was just being polite, I thought. She had probably asked because she thought *I* liked tag.

"Do you want to swing?" Jessica Farrell asked.

"Sure," I agreed.

While we were swinging, Jessica Farrell looked around the playground. "Who's the most popular kid in Mrs. Otis's class?" she asked.

"I don't know," I said.

"There must be someone," Jessica Farrell said.

"Well, maybe Elizabeth," I said. "Pretty much everyone likes her. Even the boys. And she's Student of the Week this week."

"What's Student of the Week?" Jessica asked.

I told her all about the contest.

"Who wrote about Elizabeth?" Jessica Farrell wanted to know.

"Eva," I told her.

"What did Eva say in her paper?" Jessica Farrell asked.

"Mrs. Otis doesn't tell us," I said.

"But you know, don't you?" Jessica Farrell asked. "I mean, Elizabeth is your twin sister."

I nodded.

"You can tell me," Jessica Farrell said.

"Well . . ." I said slowly.

"Go on," Jessica Farrell said.

"Oh, OK," I said. "Eva's father hurt his back. Eva was really worried. Elizabeth cheered her up."

When Eva's father was sick, it was a big secret. Elizabeth hadn't even told me about it. But now Mr. Simpson was better. I didn't think Eva would mind if Jessica Farrell knew about him. "That was nice of Elizabeth," Jessica Farrell said.

"Yeah," I agreed.

"I don't see Elizabeth," Jessica Farrell said. "Where is she?"

I held on to my swing with one hand. I pointed to where Elizabeth was jumping rope with Eva, Amy, Lois Waller, and Suzie Nichols.

"Let's go watch," Jessica Farrell suggested.

"OK," I said.

We jumped off the swings and ran over to the other girls.

Amy and Eva were turning the rope. Lois was jumping. Well, *trying* to jump.

"Hi!" Elizabeth greeted us. "Want to play?"

"Sure," I said.

Jessica Farrell nodded.

Elizabeth picked up one of her feet and wiggled it around in the air. She was wearing pink Keds, just like mine. "I'm sure I'm going to do better today. I have on my lucky shoes."

"Elizabeth, it's your turn," Suzie called.

"OK," Elizabeth said. She stood close to the swinging rope. She swayed with its beat. Then she ran in. That part went OK.

"All right!" I yelled.

Just then Elizabeth's feet got tangled. She fell.

I groaned.

Elizabeth got up. She was shaking her head.

"Hey, Elizabeth!" It was Todd. His face was red and he was sweaty. "Want to play tag?"

"OK!" Elizabeth yelled. She turned to the other girls. "I'm going to play tag. But I want to try double Dutch again tomorrow."

The others nodded.

"'Bye!" Elizabeth ran off with the boys.

"I'm tired of turning the rope," Eva announced.

"I'll do it," Lois said.

Lois and Amy got the rope going again.

"Do you want to go next?" I asked Jessica Farrell.

Jessica didn't answer. She was gone!

"Where's Jessica?" I asked Eva.

Eva shrugged.

I finally spotted Jessica Farrell. She was way across the playground. She was playing tag with Elizabeth and the boys!

I was confused. Jessica Farrell had told me she didn't like tag.

I walked over to where Ellen and Lila were playing hopscotch. I told them about what had happened.

"Told you so," Ellen said. "Jessica only *seems* nice. She isn't really."

I still didn't quite believe her.

CHAPTER 4

A Good Speller

"Please number your papers from one to ten," Mrs. Otis said that afternoon. We were getting ready for a spelling test.

"Good luck," Elizabeth whispered to me.

"You too," I said. Elizabeth didn't really need luck. She had studied the spelling words the night before.

I hadn't studied as long as Elizabeth had. But I didn't need luck, either. I am a terrific speller—even better than Elizabeth. I won the district spelling bee earlier this year.

That doesn't mean I never miss words on spelling tests. I do, all the time. But I was hoping I wouldn't miss any that day. I wanted to get an A+. If I did, the other kids might write about my spelling skills on Friday.

"I hope this isn't hard," Jessica Farrell whispered to me.

"I'm not worried," I said. "I'm a champion speller."

Jessica Farrell gave me a look like she thought I was bragging. Well, I *am* a champion speller. As soon as we got our papers back, Jessica would see.

"Let's begin," Mrs. Otis said.

The first four words were pretty hard. But I was certain I got them right.

"The next word is 'accomplish,'" Mrs. Otis said.

I wrote down my answer. I chewed on my pencil and studied what I had written. Something looked wrong. I crossed out my answer and changed it.

"The next word is 'offer,'" Mrs. Otis said.

That one was easy. I wrote my answer down quickly. Then I glanced over at Jessica Farrell. She was smiling.

When the test was over, Mrs. Otis collected our papers. "I'm going to grade these right away," she told us. "You can read quietly until I finish."

Jessica Farrell and I passed notes while everyone else read. I decided that Ellen was wrong about her cousin. Jessica Farrell was nice *and* fun. So what if she liked tag?

"Please put your books away," Mrs. Otis said a few minutes later. "I'm finished grading your papers."

Things got noisy while everyone opened and closed their desks. Mrs. Otis waited for quiet.

"I'm going to call the names of the students who got perfect papers," Mrs. Otis announced. "If I call your name, please come to the front and get a gold star."

"Cool," Jessica Farrell said.

I nodded. "I love gold stars."

"Andy," Mrs. Otis called.

Andy Franklin went up front and got his star.

"Elizabeth," Mrs. Otis called.

I smiled at Elizabeth. "Good job!"

"Thanks," Elizabeth said. She went up, got her star, and then sat back down. "I bet you get a perfect paper too," she whispered to me.

"I hope so," I said.

Mrs. Otis was flipping through the papers.

"And . . . Jess—" Mrs. Otis started to say.

All right!

While everyone watched, I jumped up and went to the front of the room. Mrs. Otis held out a star. But before I could take it, she pulled it back. "I'm sorry,"

Mrs. Otis said. "But it's the other Jessica who got a perfect paper."

My face got hot.

Almost everyone laughed as I walked back to my seat.

Jessica Farrell went up and got the star—*my* star. That made me mad.

Mrs. Otis asked Caroline Pearce to hand out the rest of the papers. When I saw mine, I got even madder. I had missed only one word—'accomplish.' I spelled it with one *C*. I missed getting a star because of one stupid letter!

"Good work," Lila told Jessica Farrell. She was on her way to sharpen her pencil.

"Thanks," Jessica Farrell said. "I feel great. I beat a champion speller!" She nodded her head toward me.

Talk about bragging!

Lila laughed.

I didn't think Jessica Farrell was funny.

CHAPTER 5

Dumb Lila

Elizabeth and I went to the park after school.

As we were getting off our bikes, Amy ran up to us. "Want to play space explorers?"

"Definitely," Elizabeth said.

I don't like space explorers. "No, thanks," I said.

"See you later!" Elizabeth ran off with Amy.

I looked around for my friends. I saw Lila sitting under a tree. I was mad at her for laughing at me after the spelling test. But none of my other friends were there. I walked over and sat down next to Lila.

"Hi," Lila said.

"Hi," I said.

We watched the other kids play for a few minutes.

"I wish I had an ice cream," Lila said.

"Do you know what I wish?" I said. "I wish Ellen's cousin was named Ann. Or Nancy. Anything but Jessica."

"I know why," Lila said. "If she had a different name, you wouldn't have looked stupid in front of the whole class."

I nodded, wishing Lila hadn't reminded me.

"Know what you should do?" Lila asked.

"What?" I asked.

"Change your name," Lila said. "Now is the perfect time. You could pick something really glamorous. Like Alexandra."

I did not like Lila's suggestion. Jessica was *my* name. It had been my name for my entire life. I didn't want to change it.

"Do you know what I think?" I asked angrily.

"What?" Lila said.

"I think the other Jessica should change her name," I said. "I was here first."

Lila shrugged.

"Besides, what's wrong with my name?" I demanded. "It's just as good as Alexandra."

Lila laughed. "No, it's not."

"Is so!" I yelled. "And it's twice as glamorous as Lila."

Lila stood up. "Is not!"

"Is so," I yelled. "Lila is just about the ugliest name in the world."

"Say you're sorry," Lila demanded.

"No!" I yelled.

Lila stomped off.

I sat down under the tree alone. After a few minutes, I started to calm down. That's when Jessica Farrell and Ellen arrived.

"Is Lila here?" Ellen asked.

"Yeah," I said. "But we had a fight. Maybe I should find her and say I'm sorry."

Ellen nodded. "Good idea."

But Jessica Farrell shook her head. "I bet Lila is still mad. It's probably not a good time to say you're sorry."

"Maybe you're right," I said. I don't like to say I'm sorry. I didn't mind putting it off for a while.

"I'll go talk to Lila," Jessica Farrell said. "After she feels better, I'll bring her back here. *Then* you can say you're sorry."

"OK," I agreed.

Ellen and I watched Jessica Farrell run off.

"Do you want to play?" I asked Ellen.

Ellen shrugged. "Not really."

"Is something wrong?" I asked.

"Jessica told me you said I'm bad at hopscotch," Ellen said.

"I didn't say that!" I exclaimed. "I said you have trouble with the number-eight square."

Ellen shrugged. "Jessica always twists the truth."

"What do you mean?" I asked.

"Jessica makes everything other people say sound bad," Ellen said. "Even if they didn't mean anything bad."

"I didn't mean anything bad," I said.

"I believe you," Ellen said. "I'm not mad."

"Come on," I said. "Let's play."

"OK," Ellen agreed.

Even though we were kind of old for it, Ellen and I played in the sandbox. We built an entire castle and destroyed it. Jessica Farrell and Lila still hadn't come back.

"What happened to them?" I wondered out loud.

"Beats me," Ellen said.

I stood up and brushed the sand off my legs. "I'm going to go look for them. Want to come?"

Ellen shook her head.

I marched off in the direction Lila and Jessica Farrell had gone. I spotted them sitting on the jungle gym. They were laughing. I was glad Lila wasn't angry anymore.

"What's so funny?" I called as I walked up to them.

"You!" Lila said.

"Me?" I repeated.

"Lila told me you thought Caroline was a witch," Jessica Farrell said. "How could you be so dumb?"

What Jessica Farrell had said was true. Last Halloween, Elizabeth and I had thought Caroline was a real witch. It had been very scary. I was

surprised—and mad. Why had Lila told Jessica Farrell about my wild imagination?

"It was an honest mistake," I said.

"Well, I'm *not* a princess," Jessica Farrell said. "Just in case you were wondering."

I didn't think that was funny at all. Lila did. She was giggling like mad.

"Jessica!" Ellen hollered from a distance. "We have to go."

Jessica Farrell jumped off the jungle gym. " 'Bye, Lila," she said.

" 'Bye," Lila said.

Jessica Farrell ran in Ellen's direction. She didn't even say good-bye to me.

I turned to Lila. "I can't believe you!" I yelled. "How could you tell Jessica about Caroline?"

"Easy!" Lila yelled. "Jessica told me you told her that I still sleep with my baby blanket."

I opened my mouth. But I didn't know what to say, so I closed it again.

"You are not my friend anymore," Lila told me.

I watched Lila stomp off for the second time that afternoon.

CHAPTER 6

The Most Popular Jessica

Before class started on Wednesday morning, Eva and Jessica Farrell went up to Mrs. Otis.

"I want to move my desk," Jessica Farrell said.

Mrs. Otis looked surprised. "Why?"

"Because I want to sit next to Eva," Jessica Farrell explained.

"Well, OK," Mrs. Otis said. She's pretty understanding about stuff like that.

Mrs. Otis got up. She asked several people to move their seats.

Lila got her desk back. I smiled at

her when she sat down next to me. She did not smile back.

Jerry McAllister moved to the end of the back row. Jessica Farrell got the desk next to Eva's.

I could hear Jessica and Eva whispering and giggling all morning. I was worried. Eva was supposed to write about me for Student of the Week. What if she wrote about Jessica Farrell instead?

Later that morning, Eva raised her hand. "May I go to the rest room?" she asked Mrs. Otis.

"Of course," Mrs. Otis said.

I quickly raised my hand. "I have to go too."

"OK," Mrs. Otis said. "You girls can go together."

Eva went out into the hallway. She didn't wait for me.

I hurried to catch up. "Hey, Eva," I said. "You're still going to write about me on Friday, aren't you?"

"No," Eva said.

"No?" I repeated. "You mean you haven't decided yet?"

"I decided," Eva said. "I'm not writing about you. You don't deserve to be Student of the Week."

"Why not?" I asked. "I'm still good at jumping rope."

"Yes," Eva said. "But you can't keep a secret."

"I can, too," I said. "Ask anyone."

"I don't have to ask," Eva said. "I already know you told Jessica Farrell about how my dad was sick. That was a secret, wasn't it?"

"Yes," I said. "But—"

"No buts," Eva said. She hurried down the hall and went into the bathroom. I walked back to the classroom alone.

I tried to do my math, but I couldn't. I tried to think of something to say to make Eva feel better. I couldn't. It was a long morning.

"Don't forget about the Student of the Week contest," Mrs. Otis said just before lunch. "You should be thinking about what you're going to write."

Lila raised her hand. "Can we write about Jessica Farrell?"

"Why not?" Mrs. Otis said. "She's a member of our class this week. OK, everyone. Line up for lunch."

Lila was in front of me in line. I hadn't spoken to her since our fight the afternoon before.

"Why did you ask Mrs. Otis that?" I demanded.

Lila shrugged and turned away. I figured she was still mad at me.

"What could you possibly write about Jessica Farrell?" I asked.

Lila turned back around and smiled at me. "I could write that she's the most popular Jessica in our class."

Tears welled up in my eyes.

I wanted to tell Elizabeth about all

46

the terrible things that had happened to me. Things that were Jessica Farrell's fault. Elizabeth always knows how to make me feel better.

I searched for Elizabeth in the line. I spotted her near the back. She was talking to Jessica Farrell!

CHAPTER 7

Answers

"Hi, Ellen." I pulled myself up onto the low wall that surrounds the playground. Ellen had been sitting there all alone.

"Hi," Ellen said sadly.

"You were right about Jessica Farrell," I told her. "She's not as nice as she seems. At first, I thought she was my friend. But now she seems like the worst enemy I've ever had."

Ellen shrugged. "That's Jessica."

"She really makes me mad," I added. "I don't understand why she's being so mean to me."

"I don't know," Ellen said. "But she's mean to me too."

"Well, she must have a reason," I said.

"I guess," Ellen agreed.

"Know what?" I said after thinking for a moment. "I think we should find out what her reason is." I jumped down off the wall. "Come on!"

Ellen jumped down. "What are you going to do?"

"You'll see," I said.

Jessica Farrell was playing tag with Elizabeth, Amy, Eva, and a bunch of the boys. I ran up to her and tapped her on the shoulder.

"What do you want?" Jessica Farrell asked. "You're not It."

"Ellen and I want to talk to you," I said. "Alone."

"Well, OK," Jessica Farrell said. "I'll be right back," she yelled to the others.

"Hurry," Elizabeth called.

Jessica Farrell and Ellen followed me to the far side of the playground. Not many kids play there.

"What is it?" Jessica Farrell asked.

"I want to know why you repeated the things I told you," I said. "You made my friends mad at me."

"So?" Jessica Farrell said.

"So I don't like it when my friends are mad!" I told her.

"So?" Jessica Farrell said.

"So you'd better stop!" I yelled.

Jessica Farrell shook her head. "You can't tell me what to do. In fact, you two had better leave me alone—or else."

"Or else what?" I asked.

"Or else I'll tell the rest of what you told me," Jessica Farrell said. "Then you won't have any friends at all."

Ellen and I didn't say anything.

"Do you promise?" Jessica Farrell asked.

"Promise," Ellen said quietly.

"Promise," I said. I don't like giving in to bullies. But I did not have a choice. I didn't want to lose any more friends.

Jessica Farrell ran back to the tag game.

Ellen put her arm around my shoulder. "Don't worry. She'll only be here for two more days."

I had a feeling it was going to be a long two days.

CHAPTER 8

Bare Feet

"Are you OK?" Elizabeth asked me after lunch. "You seem upset."

"I'm OK," I said. "But will you play with me at recess this afternoon?"

"Sure," Elizabeth said.

That made me feel much better. *Jessica Farrell might make Lila and Eva mad at me*, I thought. *But she'll never stop Elizabeth from being my best friend.*

When it was time for recess, Elizabeth, Ellen, and I lined up together. Jessica Farrell was behind us. She was standing with Eva. Mrs. Otis started to lead us outside.

"What do you want to play?" Ellen asked me and Elizabeth.

"Jump rope," Elizabeth said right away. "Double Dutch. OK?"

"Sure," I said.

Ellen nodded.

Jessica Farrell must have heard what Elizabeth said. "Can Eva and I play double Dutch with you?" she asked.

"Sure," Elizabeth said.

Ellen rolled her eyes at me. I wondered what Jessica Farrell was up to. She had told Ellen and me to stay away from her. Why wasn't she staying away from *us*?

"I'll turn the rope," Eva said when we were out on the playground.

Jessica Farrell smiled at her. "Me, too."

Eva and Jessica Farrell got the rope going.

Ellen jumped first. She fell.

I jumped. I fell.

Elizabeth jumped. She fell too. Elizabeth looked thoughtful as she got up. "I still think I'm falling because of my shoes. They're tripping me."

"But you tried changing them," I reminded her. "And it didn't help."

"I know," Elizabeth said. "That's why I want to try jumping in my bare feet."

"Really?" I asked.

"Do you think I should?" Elizabeth asked.

"Well . . ." I said.

Jessica Farrell giggled. "Do it!"

Elizabeth sat down. She quickly untied her shoes, pulled off her socks, and got up.

"Do it fast," Jessica Farrell said. "Before Mrs. Otis notices your bare feet."

Jessica Farrell and Eva began to turn the rope. Elizabeth ran in. She started to jump. For the first time, she didn't trip or stumble. A big smile spread

across her face. But then Elizabeth let out a scream. She sat down fast. She was cradling her foot.

Eva and Jessica Farrell dropped the rope.

I ran to Elizabeth's side. "What's the matter?"

Elizabeth was crying. Her foot was bloody.

I felt like I was going to cry too.

"I bet you stepped on a piece of glass," Eva told Elizabeth. "I did that at the beach once."

"It really hurts," Elizabeth sniffled.

"Hang on," I told her. "I'll get help."

Mrs. Otis was on the other side of the playground. I ran toward her as fast as I could. I wanted to get help fast.

"Mrs. Otis!" I yelled, running up to her. "Hurry! Come quick."

"What's wrong?" Mrs. Otis asked.

"It's Elizabeth," I said. "She hurt her foot."

"Where is she?" Mrs. Otis asked.

"I'll show you," I said.

I started to run across the playground. Mrs. Otis hurried after me. But she doesn't run that fast. We had only gotten about two-thirds of the way there when I saw Mr. Butler scoop Elizabeth up. He started to carry her toward the building.

I ran faster.

"Wait!" Elizabeth cried. "I want Jessica to come with me."

"I'm coming," I yelled.

But Jessica Farrell got there first. She picked up Elizabeth's shoes and hurried after Mr. Butler.

I stopped in my tracks. I knew Elizabeth had wanted *me* to come with her. How dare Jessica Farrell take my place?

The bell rang. My class lined up. Mrs. Otis let me walk at the front of the line with her.

"I'm worried," I told her.

"I'm sure Elizabeth will be fine," Mrs. Otis said.

Guess who was waiting for us in the classroom? Elizabeth and Jessica Farrell!

I ran up to them. "Are you OK?" I asked Elizabeth.

Elizabeth smiled and nodded. "I'm fine. Eva was right. I stepped on a piece of glass. The nurse had to take it out."

"It really bled a lot," Jessica Farrell added. Then she smiled at Elizabeth and went over to talk to Eva.

"Did you miss me in the nurse's office?" I asked Elizabeth.

"A little," Elizabeth admitted.

I put my hands on my hips. "Jessica Farrell makes me so mad. How could she take my place like that?"

"Don't be mad," Elizabeth said. "Jessica came to the nurse's office because she was worried about me. I think that was nice. In fact, I'm going to write about it on Friday."

I rolled my eyes. My own sister wanted Jessica Farrell to be Student of the Week?

CHAPTER 9

Lost Elizabeth

"I can't wait to get to your house," Ellen told me after school. "It will be great to get away from Jessica."

"I know," I said. "I just wish we could get away from her *right now*."

Ellen and I were standing in the school yard waiting for Elizabeth. She was talking to Jessica Farrell and Ellen's older sister, Debbie, on the steps. Jessica Farrell and Debbie were waiting for Mrs. Riteman to pick them up. Debbie and Ellen usually ride our bus. But Mrs. Riteman had been driving the girls to and from school that week.

Elizabeth had been hanging around Jessica Farrell ever since she cut her foot. She acted like Jessica was some kind of hero or something. It made me mad.

"Come on," I said to Ellen. "Let's get on the bus. Elizabeth can catch up."

"OK," Ellen said.

The two of us got onto the bus. Steven and his friends were sitting in the back. The seat Elizabeth and I usually sit in was empty. I plopped down.

"Sit next to me," I told Ellen.

"Where will Elizabeth sit?" Ellen asked.

I shrugged. "I don't care."

Ellen sat down. "Are you mad at Elizabeth?"

"A little," I said. "I don't want her to be friends with Jessica Farrell."

Ellen nodded. "I can understand that. I wasn't happy when you were all buddy-buddy with her, either."

"Yeah," I said. "I remember."

"Are they still on the steps?" Ellen asked.

I pressed my nose against the window. "I don't see them." The yard was almost empty. Most of the kids had got their rides or got onto a bus.

"I hope Elizabeth doesn't miss the bus," Ellen said.

At that moment, the bus driver closed the door.

"Wait!" I yelled. "Don't leave yet. My sister isn't here."

"That may be, but it's time to go," the bus driver said.

"But we can't leave without her," I yelled.

"If she's late, we can," the driver said.

Steven came down the aisle. "Hey, you have to wait for my sister! She's just a little kid."

I usually don't like it when Steven

calls me and Elizabeth little kids. But this time I was glad. The bus driver listened to Steven. He opened the bus door. "I'll give her a few minutes," the bus driver said.

"Where do you think she is?" Ellen asked me.

I was staring out the window. "I don't know." My tummy was starting to feel funny. What had happened to Elizabeth?

A minute passed. And then another. And another.

The kids on the bus started to act up. One of Steven's friends was throwing spitballs. Some of the first-graders were bouncing on their seats. Everyone was making lots of noise.

The bus driver closed the door.

"I think he's leaving," Ellen said.

"Don't leave!" I yelled.

"I'm sorry," the bus driver called back. "But we're already late. If I don't get the rest of you kids home, your parents will be worried." He pulled away from the curb.

"This is terrible," Ellen said. "Where do you think Elizabeth is?"

"I don't know," I said. "But I'm really worried."

"Maybe she was kidnapped," Caroline Pearce said.

"Shut up," Ellen told her.

After the first stop, Steven slid into the seat behind us. "Where's Elizabeth?"

"I don't know!" I exclaimed. "Something terrible must have happened to her."

"Don't worry," Steven said. "We'll tell Mom as soon as we get home. She'll know what to do."

It felt as if a long time passed before the bus got to our stop. When it finally did, Steven, Ellen, and I were the first ones off. We ran all the way home.

"Mommy! Mommy!" I yelled as we ran into the house.

Mom came out of the kitchen. Soapy water was dripping from her hands. "What's the matter?"

"Elizabeth is missing," I cried.

"The bus driver left without her," Steven added.

Mom shook her head and smiled. "It's OK, kids. Elizabeth is fine. She just called. She's over at the Ritemans'."

"What's she doing at my house?" Ellen asked.

"Playing with your cousin," Mom explained.

I couldn't believe it. Elizabeth had gone to the Ritemans' without telling me! I was mad. Why hadn't Elizabeth told me where she was going? And why had she gone somewhere I wasn't invited?

CHAPTER 10

A Big Fat Lie

Later that afternoon, Mrs. Riteman came to pick Ellen up. She dropped Elizabeth off at the same time. Elizabeth came straight up to our room. I was lying in bed, playing with my stuffed koala bear.

"Hi," Elizabeth said brightly. "I had a great time at the Ritemans'. Did you have fun with Ellen?"

"No," I said.

Elizabeth sat down on my bed. "Why not?"

"Because of you," I said.

"Me?" Elizabeth looked confused. "But I wasn't even here."

"Right!" I said. "And you didn't tell me where you were going, either. Ellen and I were really worried when you didn't get on the bus. Even Steven was worried! How could you go to the Ritemans' without inviting me?"

"But Jessica Farrell invited you," Elizabeth said. "She said you didn't want to come."

I sat up. "That's a big fat lie!" I yelled. "Jessica Farrell did not invite me. She wouldn't."

"Are you saying Jessica Farrell lied?" Elizabeth asked.

"Absolutely!" I said.

"Don't be silly," Elizabeth said. "Jessica Farrell wouldn't do that."

"Either she's lying or I am," I said. "Who do you believe?"

Elizabeth didn't say anything.

"*Her?*" I asked.

Elizabeth shrugged.

"I'm not lying!" I yelled.

69

"Can you prove it?" Elizabeth asked.

I didn't answer. Elizabeth had really hurt my feelings. Why should I prove to my own twin sister that I was telling the truth?

"No, I can't," I told Elizabeth. "Just forget it."

"Don't be mad," Elizabeth said. "Listen, I was going to start my homework. But we could play instead."

"Do your homework," I said. I wasn't about to play with Elizabeth. Let her go play with Jessica Farrell!

I went downstairs. Mom was making dinner.

"Can I call Ellen?" I asked.

Mom looked surprised. "But she just left."

"I know," I said. "But I really, really need to talk to her."

"Well, OK," Mom said. "But don't talk long. It's almost time for dinner." Mom dialed the phone and handed it to me.

"Hello?" came a grown-up voice. I think it was Mr. Riteman.

"Hello," I said. "This is Jessica Wakefield. May I speak to Ellen, please?"

"Hang on," said the voice.

A minute passed.

"Jessica?" It was Ellen. "I just got home."

"I know," I said. "Listen, I decided it's time to teach Jessica Farrell a lesson."

"But we promised to leave her alone," Ellen said.

"I don't care," I said. "Will you help me?"

"OK," Ellen agreed.

"Great," I said. "Now here's the plan. . . ."

CHAPTER 11

Twin Switch

"I'm sorry I got mad at you yesterday," I told Elizabeth on Thursday morning.

Elizabeth smiled. "Really? I'm glad."

"I have an idea," I said. "Let's wear the same outfit to school today."

"OK," Elizabeth said. "You can pick our outfit."

"Let's wear pink sweatshirts and blue shorts," I suggested.

"Sounds good." Elizabeth nodded.

We got dressed in our identical outfits. I even put my hair in a ponytail to match Elizabeth's.

When we got to school, the classroom was full. Everyone was running around, laughing and talking. Mrs. Otis wasn't there yet.

Ellen was standing just inside the door.

"Hi," she said to Elizabeth as soon as we walked in. "I just got a new book about horses. Want to see it?"

"Sure," Elizabeth said eagerly.

When Elizabeth turned her back, I gave Ellen the thumbs-up. Then I looked around the room for Jessica Farrell. She was sitting in my desk. I knew she was waiting for my sister. I made myself smile. Then I sat down at Elizabeth's desk.

"Hi!" I said cheerfully.

"Hi!" Jessica Farrell said.

"I really had fun yesterday afternoon," I said.

Jessica Farrell smiled. She thought I was Elizabeth! "I had fun too."

"Too bad you have to leave soon," I said.

"I know," Jessica Farrell said. "My friends at home aren't half as much fun as you."

The room suddenly quieted down. Mrs. Otis had come in.

"I want to ask Mrs. Otis a question," I told Jessica Farrell. "I'll be right back."

"OK, Elizabeth," Jessica Farrell said.

I skipped to the front of the room. My plan was working perfectly!

"Thanks for letting me see your book," Elizabeth was telling Ellen. "I think I'd better sit down now."

Ellen glanced at me. I nodded.

"OK," Ellen said. "See you."

Elizabeth sat down in her seat. Jessica Farrell gave her a dirty look. Then she glanced up at me and smiled. Hurray! She still thought I was Elizabeth. I crept closer so I could hear what was happening.

"Why are you talking to me?" Jessica Farrell was saying to Elizabeth. "I told you to leave me alone."

"What?" Elizabeth said. "Why would you tell me that?"

"You know why," Jessica Farrell said. "Because if you don't, I'm going to tell everyone the secrets you told me."

Elizabeth looked confused. "What secrets?" she asked.

"Come off it, Jessica," Jessica Farrell said. "You know what I'm talking about."

"I do *not* know what you're talking about," Elizabeth said. "And I'm Elizabeth."

I went and stood beside my sister. "And I'm Jessica."

Jessica Farrell looked shocked for about a second. Then she turned to Elizabeth and laughed. "I was just joking," she said. "Right, Jessica?"

I shook my head.

Eva, Lila, and Ellen had come up behind me.

"I don't think you were joking," Elizabeth said. "It wasn't funny."

"She wasn't joking," Ellen said. "That's how she always talks to me."

"How could you be so mean?" Eva asked.

Jessica Farrell started to cry. "I only did it because I wanted you guys to be my friends."

"Just because you want friends doesn't mean you can take them away from me," I said.

"Or me," Ellen added.

"But I had to make you angry at Jessica and Ellen," Jessica Farrell told Lila, Eva, and Elizabeth. "Otherwise, you wouldn't have had time to play with me."

"That's not true," Lila said.

"I have time for lots of friends," Elizabeth told her.

"Really?" Jessica Farrell asked.

Elizabeth nodded. "But not ones that lie."

Jessica Farrell wiped her eyes. "I'll try to stop lying," she said. "I promise."

"Let's get started," Mrs. Otis called.

We took our seats.

"I'm sorry I thought you lied," Elizabeth whispered to me.

"That's OK," I said. "Jessica Farrell tricked me for a while, too."

Mrs. Otis passed out some math worksheets. Elizabeth and I started to do ours. After a while, Elizabeth leaned toward me.

"Don't you feel sorry for Jessica Farrell?" she asked.

"No," I said.

"I do," Elizabeth said. "I think we should give her another chance."

I frowned. "Maybe . . ." I said.

Lila leaned over from the other side. "I still wish you hadn't told Jessica

Farrell about my blanket," she said. "But I guess you didn't mean to make fun of me. I'm not mad at you anymore."

"Thanks," I said.

Eva sits way in the back. I turned around to look at her. She smiled.

I was starting to feel much better.

CHAPTER 12

Victory!

"Here they come," I told Elizabeth.

Ellen and Jessica Farrell were walking across the playground together. They were laughing. Elizabeth and I called hello to them.

"Hi!" Ellen said as they came up to us.

"Hi." Jessica Farrell seemed almost shy.

"Guess what we just found out," Ellen said.

"What?" Elizabeth asked.

"Jessica likes dogs," Ellen said. "And she likes fireworks. Two of my favorite things!"

I narrowed my eyes.

Jessica Farrell noticed the look on my face. "I know what you're thinking," she said. "First I pretended to like the things you like. Then I pretended to like the things Elizabeth likes. But this is different. I really do like dogs and fireworks. Promise."

"We believe you," Elizabeth said. "Right, Jessica?"

"Right," I said. Elizabeth had made me promise to give Jessica Farrell another chance. But I still wasn't sure.

"Know what else?" Jessica Farrell said.

"What?" I asked.

"Ellen and I have the same middle name!" Jessica Farrell announced.

That made me smile. "No wonder you two have so much in common!"

"Jessica, I'm sorry I was mean to you," Jessica Farrell said. "Can we be friends again?"

"Well . . ." I said.

Elizabeth, Ellen, and Jessica Farrell were all looking at me. "Sure," I decided.

"Great," Jessica Farrell said.

"Let's play hopscotch together later," I suggested to Jessica Farrell as Mrs. Otis led us into the school.

Jessica Farrell wrinkled her nose. "I hate hopscotch."

At first, I was a little angry. But then I laughed. Jessica really *had* stopped lying.

"You can play tag with me instead," Elizabeth suggested.

"OK!" Jessica Farrell agreed.

"Maybe we can eat lunch together," I suggested.

"That would be fun," Jessica Farrell said. "I'll even share my sandwich with you. It's tuna salad."

"Do you like tuna salad?" I asked. "I know you told me you did, but do you *really*?"

"Love it," Jessica Farrell said.

I smiled at Jessica Farrell. I felt as if I were meeting her for the first time. And even though she didn't like everything I did, I liked *her*.

We went into the room and sat down. Mrs. Otis took attendance. Then she gave us each a piece of paper. "It's time for you to write your Student of the Week papers," she told us.

I stared at my paper. I had been busy all week trying to talk my friends into writing about me. I hadn't spent any time thinking about who *I* was going to write about.

Elizabeth? No. She had won the week before.

Ellen? She *had* been a good friend all week.

But then I decided to write about Ellen next week. This time I wrote about Jessica Farrell.

I was a little surprised at myself. But

Jessica Farrell had learned some important stuff that week. She'd learned how to be herself. She learned not to lie. I thought that was pretty cool.

Mrs. Otis collected the papers. We did math problems while she read them. After a while, Mrs. Otis told us to put our pencils down. "I'm ready to announce the Student of the Week," she said.

The class grew quiet.

"It's Jessica Farrell," Mrs. Otis said.

Lila gasped. Even Elizabeth looked surprised.

But I was grinning.

Later that morning, Mrs. Otis pinned a photograph of Jessica Farrell on the bulletin board. My picture was right next to hers.

"Thanks," Jessica Farrell told me.

"Hey, anytime," I said.

At lunch, Elizabeth played tag with Jessica Farrell for a while. Then she

came over to play double Dutch with me. Elizabeth still kept falling. Finally, I suggested we jump together. Elizabeth and I held hands and ran into the rope. We jumped and jumped and jumped. We even ran out without falling.

Elizabeth was laughing. "That was great! It must be because we're twins."

"Or maybe it's because you kept your shoes on," I said.

The next day, Elizabeth and I rode our bikes to the park.

Ellen was there.

"Did Jessica Farrell leave?" I asked.

Ellen nodded. "This morning. I miss her."

"It *is* quiet around here," I agreed.

"Not for long." Elizabeth turned to Ellen. "Our mom and dad just told us they're taking us to the circus soon."

"My family is going too," Ellen said.

"I can't wait. I love the clowns."

"Me too," Elizabeth agreed. "But I really want to see the pony riders."

I wrinkled my nose. "I'm not going to like that part."

"Why not?" Elizabeth asked.

"Because pony riders ride *ponies*," I said. "And ponies stink." I held my nose.

Elizabeth laughed. "Ponies don't smell *that* bad. I think you might be surprised."

I shrugged. "Maybe."

Will Jessica like the pony riders at the circus? Find out in Sweet Valley Kids #60, *The Amazing Jessica*.

SIGN UP FOR THE SWEET VALLEY HIGH® FAN CLUB!

Hey, girls! Get all the gossip on Sweet Valley High's® most popular teenagers when you join our fantastic Fan Club! As a member, you'll get all of this really cool stuff:

- Membership Card with your own personal Fan Club ID number
- A Sweet Valley High® Secret Treasure Box
- Sweet Valley High® Stationery
- Official Fan Club Pencil (for secret note writing!)
- Three Bookmarks
- A "Members Only" Door Hanger
- Two Skeins of J. & P. Coats® Embroidery Floss with flower barrette instruction leaflet
- Two editions of *The Oracle* newsletter
- Plus exclusive Sweet Valley High® product offers, special savings, contests, and much more!

Be the first to find out what Jessica & Elizabeth Wakefield are up to by joining the Sweet Valley High® Fan Club for the one-year membership fee of only $6.25 each for U.S. residents, $8.25 for Canadian residents (U.S. currency). Includes shipping & handling.

Send a check or money order (do not send cash) made payable to "Sweet Valley High® Fan Club" along with this form to:

SWEET VALLEY HIGH® FAN CLUB, BOX 3919-B, SCHAUMBURG, IL 60168-3919

NAME_____

(Please print clearly)

ADDRESS_____

CITY_____ STATE _____ ZIP_____

(Required)

AGE_____ BIRTHDAY_____ / _____ / _____

Offer good while supplies last. Allow 6-8 weeks after check clearance for delivery. Addresses without ZIP codes cannot be honored. Offer good in USA & Canada only. Void where prohibited by law.

SWEET VALLEY KIDS

Jessica and Elizabeth have had lots of adventures in *Sweet Valley High* and *Sweet Valley Twins*...now read about the twins at age seven! You'll love all the fun that comes with being seven—birthday parties, playing dress-up, class projects, putting on puppet shows and plays, losing a tooth, setting up lemonade stands, caring for animals and much more! It's all part of SWEET VALLEY KIDS. Read them all!